Great Morning
with a Missing Bright, Shiny Pink Ribbon

PAGE PUBLISHING, INC.
New York, NY

First originally published by Page Publishing, Inc. 2018

ISBN 978-1-64214-746-9 (Paperback)
ISBN 978-1-64214-747-6 (Digital)

Printed in the United States of America

Great Morning
with a Missing Bright, Shiny Pink Ribbon

DONNA ARENA

Hi, my name is Morning! Mom says that every day the morning sun gives you a new chance to show the world how great you are. That's why she called me "Morning"!

Some days are really great, but other days are not. I try to make those days great too! Mom helps with this a lot. Come along with me, friends, as I share one of those days with you!

It was one of the best school days of the year. It was time to sing for concert day! Singing is so much fun! *La la la la la*!

5

I just loved my new dress for the concert. Mom bought a bright, shiny pink ribbon for my hair. It looked so pretty with the flowers on my dress. Pink is the best color ever!

I was ready for my big day, so I went to get my special pink ribbon. I thought I left it on my dresser, but then it wasn't there! "Oh no! Where can my pretty, shiny pink ribbon be? I must find it! Time to make a plan!" I said.

I called all my stuffed animals together so they could help me look. "You were in here all night," I said. "Did anyone see my bright, shiny pink ribbon?"

I asked them, but their faces did not give a clue!

Is it inside my dresser? NO!

Is it under my bed? NO!

Is it in the closet? NO!

In the kitchen? NO!

In the refrigerator? NO!

In my old, smelly sneaker? No, no, and NO!"

13

I began to think about what could have happened to my ribbon.

Maybe a bird flew in during the night, took my bright, shiny pink ribbon, and flew away with it! The bird thought it was a worm, and ate it all up!

Maybe the wind blew it out the window, and it's sitting on top of a tall tree right now! My poor ribbon! It doesn't even have a sweater or hat!

Maybe my ribbon met my socks, and they are all having a dance party right now!

My socks do love to dance when they're on my feet!

I asked Mom if she saw my ribbon, and guess what she held up? She was holding my bright, shiny pink ribbon!

"My ribbon!" I screamed so loud I think I scared my stuffed animals! "I thought the birds ate it, or it was stuck in a tall tree, or dancing with socks!" I told Mom.

"Of course not, Morning. I took it to make sure you didn't lose it," Mom explained.

"I'm so happy," I said. "I couldn't sing today without my ribbon!" I asked my stuffed animals, "Are you sure you didn't see Mom take the ribbon?"

I think they knew, but they didn't want to tell on Mom!

"Morning," Mom said, "Your concert will be great with or without your ribbon. Remember that every day the morning sun gives you a new chance to show the world how great you are. You are great, Morning, and not because of your bright, shiny pink ribbon. You are great because you're you."

"Thanks, Mom," I said. "And my ribbon is great too!"

ABOUT THE AUTHOR

Donna Arena is a certified teacher and mother of two. She has over two decades of classroom experience, ranging from elementary teaching to community, volunteer teaching. Her greatest joy in the classroom has been appreciating entertaining stories with her students. Donna is thrilled to introduce her book _Great Morning with a Missing Bright, Shiny Pink Ribbon._ Her wish is for children to meet laughter and hope as they discover this book.